Cleans Up

Jorge el curioso
limpia el reguero

LIBRO BILINGÜE EN ESPAÑOL E INGLÉS

Adaptación de Stephen Krensky
Traducido por Yanitzia Canetti
Basado en un guión para una serie de televisión
escrito por Joe Fallon

Houghton Mifflin Company
Boston 2007

Adaptation by Stephen Krensky
Translated by Yanitzia Canetti
Based on the TV series teleplay written by Joe Fallon

For information about permission to reproduce selections from this book, write to Permissions, Houghton Mifflin Company, 215 Park Avenue South, New York, New York 10003.

Library of Congress Cataloging-in-Publication data is on file.

Design by Joyce White

www.houghtonmifflinbooks.com

Manufactured in Singapore
TWP 10 9 8 7 6
4500290348

It was an exciting day.
A new rug had arrived.
George was curious to
see if it would fit.

Fue un día emocionante.
Llegó una alfombra nueva.
Jorge estaba curioso por ver
cómo iba a quedar.

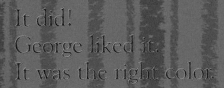

It did!
George liked it.
It was the right color.

¡Quedó muy bien!
A Jorge le gustaba.
Tenía el color adecuado.

It was soft to walk on.
The rug was just perfect.

¡Y qué suavecita!
Era la alfombra perfecta.

All that walking made George thirsty.
He poured himself a big glass of grape juice.

Con tanta actividad, a Jorge le dio sed.
Así que se sirvió un vaso grande de jugo de uva.

Then he went back to the rug.
It felt squishy between his toes.

Luego regresó a la alfombra.
Se sentía esponjosa entre sus patitas.

George thought it would
be fun to jump on the rug.
So he jumped.

Jorge pensó que sería divertido
saltar en la alfombra.
Así que saltó.

George forgot about
the grape juice.
It jumped, too.

A Jorge se le olvidó que
tenía un vaso lleno de jugo de uva.
Y el vaso también saltó.

What a mess!
George had to get that juice
off the rug.

¡Qué desastre!
Jorge tenía que quitar
ese jugo de la alfombra.

He used paper towels first.
They did not work.

Primero usó toallas de papel.
Pero no funcionó.

George remembered soap
was good for cleaning.
If one soap was good, many
soaps would be even better.

**Jorge recordó que el jabón
era bueno para limpiar.
Si un jabón era bueno, muchos
jabones serían aún mejor.**

Now all George needed was water.

Ahora todo lo que Jorge necesitaba era agua.

Maybe he used too much.

Tal vez usó demasiada.

George went to borrow a water pump from a nearby farm.

Jorge tomó prestada
la bomba de agua
de una granja cercana.

It was heavy, so he had
to put it on wheels,
And he had to get help
towing it home.

Era pesada, así que tuvo
que ponerla sobre ruedas.
Y tuvo que conseguir ayuda
para trasladarla a casa.

He used the pump a long time.
Finally there was more water
outside than inside.

**Bombeó el agua por un buen rato.
Y al final había más agua afuera
que adentro.**

When George was done, the rug
was cleaner than ever.

Cuando Jorge terminó, la alfombra
quedó más limpia que nunca.

The whole room was cleaner,
even if it was a little wet.

Toda la sala quedó más limpia,
aunque un poquito mojada.

But it took a while for everything to be perfect again.

Pero tuvo que esperar un poco más para que todo volviera a la normalidad.

SIMPLE TOOLS AND TECHNOLOGY

Curious George gets into trouble easily, but he always manages to find a way to fix things. In Cleans Up, he solves the problem with the help of a few simple tools. The pump was too heavy for him to lift or carry, so he used wheels and a rope for towing to help him reduce the pump's weight. What would you do in the following situation to help you solve the problem?

THINK ABOUT IT

You have a very heavy box of books that you need to move across the room without carrying it in your arms the whole way. You have the following materials: a rope, a large, flat board of plywood, several plastic logs, and a helper. How would you do it? (See possible solutions below.)

1) You put the wood on the logs, and the box on the wood. As one of you pushes the box and board over the logs, the other keeps moving the last log to the front edge of the plywood to keep your board moving. 2) You tie the rope to the box and both of you pull it. 3) You move the books a few at a time! Are there any more solutions?

HOW IT WORKS

Curious George used a water pump to get water from one place to another. The reason the water pump worked was because the pump created an area of low air pressure inside itself. The high pressure outside the pump pushed the water up to fill the area of low air pressure. Then the pump drained the water out its other end.

HERE ARE TWO SIMPLE EXPERIMENTS WITH AIR PRESSURE

1. Stick a paper towel inside a jar and secure it with tape. Now fill your sink with water. Flip the jar upside down and plunge it into the water until it hits the bottom. Drain the sink. Did your paper towel get wet? Can you think why?

2. Insert a straw into a full glass of water. Place one finger over the top end and lift the straw out of the glass. Does the water fall out the bottom end? Now remove your finger. What happens to the water?

Explanations: 1) The air pressure inside the glass jar did not allow the water to enter the jar at all, keeping your paper towel dry. 2) When you held your finger over the straw, you lowered the air pressure on top of the straw. The higher air pressure at the bottom of the straw kept the water from falling out. Similarly, when you drink through a straw, you are not really sucking the liquid up. You are removing the air from the straw, lowering the pressure inside it. The greater air pressure outside the straw pushes water up into your mouth. It works just like George's pump!